written by
HOLLY ROBINSON PEETE
and RJ PEETE

co-written and pictures by
SHANE W. EVANS

scholastic press • new york

When you're a kid like me, you see the world in special ways. Loud noises can hurt. Looking people in the eye can be a struggle. Making friends isn't always easy.

Having a twin sister helps.

Callie and I are the same in so many ways.

We share lots of things.

Like family days at the lake.

Counting fish and then letting the tides tickle our toes.

But for all the ways my sister and I are the same,

we're different, too.

Callie likes playdates. I like puzzles.

Callie knows all about floating boats.

I'm a fish expert.

My sister lets me be me.

Quiet. Exploring. Wishing. Wondering.

I have autism. Callie doesn't.

We're good at different things.

Mommy says when you put me near water, I shine.

The way I see — and feel — it is, wet places, spaces,

and water worlds unlock something deep inside.

Water makes my heart smile.

When the clouds spill their gifts, we're showered with blessings. With Callie, drizzles and drops don't bring on the blues. Singing in the rain is a two-part harmony.

"One, two, three . . .
kerplop, Callie!"

"Time for a puddle
party, Charlie!"

Rain-soaked toes are
no problem for Callie and me.

Big pools and lots of swimming lessons are my good buddies.

That water is a warm hug, ready to catch me the minute I jump in.

Backstroke. Fun-stroke. Float-stroke. Charlie-stroke.

Callie sings, "Charlie, you're my guppy brother!"

My favorite part is when Callie and I play a holding-hands game,

while my sister shouts, "Get ready, Olympics.

Here comes Gold Medal Charlie!"

Yes, here I come!

I have autism.

But autism doesn't

have me.

Watery ways let me

know I'm safe.

Making a splash

sets me free.

Callie and I kick back, close our eyes,

make big wishes, dream big, and let our thoughts

drift . . . glide . . . fly . . .

Water settles me down
opens me up,
takes me to places
only I can touch.

When we visit the aquarium, wonder wraps me up.

Swirls me around. Fills me with its flickering

whispers of light.

My family calls me The Fish Fact Kid.

I know the scientific names

of every fin, flipper, and gill.

It's true — fish do have lips.

That's why I blow them a kiss, as I get up close to the glass.

When you're a kid like me, silly seal faces let

your heart wave hello.

It's fun to know fish facts when snorkeling brings me nose-to-nose with Callie. My sister is as sparkly as a neon tetra.

In the mighty blue sea, I'm super smart me.

Making a splash — *yippeeee*!

At home, running water makes my fingers feel so fine.

It tickles, splishes, and gets my pinkies, thumbs,

and knuckles clean.

What's my favorite snack time drink? A tall glass of water hits the spot just fine.

"Charlie, Callie, time for your bath," Daddy calls.

Before the tub is halfway full, I sink down in, letting

the warm flow tickle my skin.

"Harriet, wait your turn. Doggie wash, up next."

When you're a kid like me, suds and bubbles are your

best friends, who make you want to stay all day.

Especially when we get

to singing our rubber ducky and

toy boat deep-down-fun ditty song.

When I get wet, I feel happy

strong, still, calm.

When you're a kid like me, family time, giggle games, and just being together, are like swimming in an ocean of love. Making the biggest splashes ever.

WHY WE WROTE THIS BOOK — AND HOW IT CAN HELP YOU

by Holly Robinson Peete

When my family collaborated on the picture book *My Brother Charlie* and the middle-grade book *Same But Different: Teen Life on the Autism Express*, we offered each as a gift to families navigating the life journey with autism, and to those who have no connection to autism but have friends who do. The outpouring of love and the personal stories of others like us who had found joy while managing the challenges of autism were overwhelming examples of what it means to be members of a community — a world of people whose experiences are similar to those of our family. I have encountered some of the most beautiful and extraordinary people on this journey, who have enriched our lives.

Charlie Makes a Splash is a companion to our previous books. In creating this narrative, it was very important that RJ, my eldest son and the twin brother to my daughter, Ryan, be the one to tell his story. Here, RJ shares his lived experience of growing up with autism. For years, he's been eager to tell readers how, in water, he finds solace, confidence, comfort, joy, and sensorial bliss.

Our first book was co-authored by my daughter, Ryan Elizabeth. *My Brother Charlie* was told from a sister's perspective. The characters Callie and Charlie are based on Ryan and RJ. In that story, young Callie acknowledges that while it hasn't always been easy for her to be Charlie's twin, she advocates lovingly for her brother.

Like our previous titles, *Charlie Makes a Splash* celebrates how special all children are, and how every one of us can find value and see amazing qualities in the uniqueness of people.

How It All Began

My son RJ was born two minutes before his twin sister, Ryan. Both newborns were beautiful, and when they arrived, like every mother, I was filled with a joy that is beyond description. RJ and Ryan were very talkative toddlers. I will always remember this, because one day, RJ's chattiness stopped, almost suddenly. I noticed, too, that while Ryan continued to pass several developmental milestones, RJ ceased making eye contact and wouldn't answer me when I called him.

In 2000, when RJ was three, we got the diagnosis of autism. I felt a profound sense of hopelessness, confusion, and anger. My husband, Rodney, and I refer to that as the "never" day, since we were told by a doctor that RJ would never accomplish so many things. The two nevers that were the most painful were that he would never verbally connect with us in a spontaneous fashion and would never say he loved us without being prompted.

I immediately plunged into overdrive, looking for ways to help him and also methods for managing our family life. There was so much that I didn't know and that I would only learn over time. Some days, I felt very alone and isolated as a parent. Autism can take a big toll on a family, emotionally, spiritually, and financially.

The medical community defines autism as a neurobiological disorder. The Centers for Disease Control and Prevention issued some startling statistics on the disorder: As of this book's publication, one in fifty-four children in the United States has an autism spectrum disorder. As more knowledge is gained, these statistics continue to change over time, with an increase in children identified with the condition. These are staggering statistics, but they show me that there are many other parents and families dealing with the same challenges. As the mother of four children, and as a wife, my life can be pretty full at times, especially given that RJ has required so many special treatments and interventions to help him as he's grown.

Very early on, we discovered that RJ finds tremendous empowerment in and around water. From the time he was of preschool age, he took to swimming, baths, beach trips, aquarium visits, and playing in the rain in the same way, well, a fish takes to water. In fact, when he was a young child, I often called RJ "my little fish." He started swim class very early to ensure his safety around water, and even though the other kids in the swim class were less verbally challenged than RJ was at the time, he was always the most efficient and fearless swimmer!

Visits to the aquarium were among the most empowering environments for RJ. To this day, when he is at the aquarium, with the muted blue light and insulated sound, my boy experiences such joy! I soon learned that watery environments are soothing sensory havens for many kids with autism.

RJ is twenty-three years old now, and he's taught me many special lessons. One that he said best as a young boy was this: "I may have autism, but autism doesn't have me!"

Indeed — autism doesn't own us. It keeps us on our toes, for sure, but when I keep RJ's mantra in mind, I'm able to get some balanced perspective, even on some of the most challenging days. As a young adult, RJ is funny, bright, adventurous, and full of insights.

Over the years, with the help of many caring professionals and a whole supportive community we call "Team RJ," our son has checked many nevers off his list. Like most parents, my husband and I continue to do everything we can to aid RJ's progress. He continues to delight us with his humor, charm, and unique perspective on things.

Now that I have some experience in raising a child with autism, I've come up with tools that I have found helpful in managing it, and in keeping our family life balanced.

Ditch the Denial

It can be tough to face the fact that our loved one may have an autism diagnosis. But as with any developmental issue, things only get worse when we pretend they don't exist. If, for any reason, you suspect your child or a loved one has autism, or if a medical professional gives you such a diagnosis, trust your gut — don't ignore it. Arm yourself with information. Early intervention is key!

Diagnosis Inequity

African American and Hispanic children tend to be diagnosed much later than Caucasian children (some-times 2–5 years later). There are several reasons for this. One is that children of color are more likely to be raised in families who are economically challenged and who have limited access to expensive resources and diagnostics. Also, because these families may not recognize signs of autism in their children, developmental milestones are often misunderstood. Also, in some cultures, there remain social stigmas about mental health and embarrassment about discussing these subjects openly. Families feel ashamed or too proud to seek help. I encourage all families to come together in their communities, schools, and places of worship to share and support the development of grassroots programs for getting and disseminating information.

Share the 411 with Family and Friends

Autism is very misunderstood in our culture. With as much effort as there has been nationally to create autism awareness and acceptance, we still have so much misinformation. Help your loved one who has an autism diagnosis by being an advocate for them. I have found tough love to be very effective, especially during family gatherings, special occasions, or holidays — tough love for my guests, that is! When RJ was much younger, we struggled through some challenging Thanksgivings, Christmases, and birthday parties. We had some family members who weren't familiar with RJ's behavior and became unhinged when he flapped his arms, cried, or screeched. At that time, we were uncomfortable, too, because we weren't completely open about his autism. We soon learned the importance of preparing both RJ and our guests in advance by telling them what they might expect. When you know better, you do better.

Give Up the Guilt

Like every mother, I worry about the well-being of my children. When you have a child with autism or any special needs, the worry can be tenfold. This is compounded by sleepless nights spent asking myself if I'm "doing the right thing" on behalf of my son. Or what happens when I am gone. Who will protect my child? But I've learned a valuable lesson. Guilt, remorse, and worry — while totally understandable — have no value and impede my ability to make smart decisions that can help RJ and my other children. So I encourage parents to drop the "G-word" from their vocabulary. It's a waste of time and counterproductive. Instead, focus on empowering your family by becoming advocates.

Siblings

Autism can have a serious effect on siblings. Children with autism can sometimes spoil playdates or be the cause for delaying or canceling family outings, due to a sibling's public meltdown. Because children with autism require so much special attention from a caregiver, siblings of kids with autism can feel neglected or even jealous when life seems to be planned exclusively around the affected child. Then, too, there is a social stigma attached to having a sibling who's different. This can be devastating. Find one-on-one time with your other kids that is built around them and them exclusively. They need to feel seen.

Self-Care Is Health Care

With any caregiving scenario, we parents take on a lot. It is imperative to find some time for self-care. Yoga and meditation are my go-tos. Find something to center yourself and set an intention for your day to help you effectively take care of others. Stress is real and powerful. Discover the best ways for you to relieve it.

Acceptance and Advocacy

As I reflect on the more than twenty years since our diagnosis, one thing I know for sure is that I wouldn't change RJ for the world, but I will always try to change the world to be a kinder place for RJ!

A WORD FROM RJ

I love my family. They understand me. They have fought for me. My goal with this book is to let kids and their parents know that kids with autism have real feelings, even though we can't always express them. I remember when I could not speak much. Now I can't stop talking!

Though some kids with autism can't speak, it doesn't mean they don't have a lot to say. Thanks to technology, many kids can communicate their thoughts and feelings. When I was less verbal, I remember hearing people talk about me or for me but not to me. That bothered me. I remember trying to talk, but it felt like I had a ball stuck in my throat. It was frustrating.

I remember wanting to tell my mom that when I went to the barbershop, it felt like lion claws on my scalp. Instead, I just roared like a lion! I am very proud of *Charlie Makes a Splash* because I get to express myself!

When we were kids, my sister, Ryan, and I put together a program for my fourth-grade class called "Autism 101." Here are some tips we think were helpful:

- If someone who has autism doesn't respond right away, doesn't make eye contact when you speak to them, or doesn't want to be touched, it doesn't mean they're being rude. Socializing can be challenging and make a child anxious.

- Many people have trouble making friends, but it's even harder for kids with autism. People who have autism sometimes stop trying to be friendly after only a short time. Include people with autism even more than you would others.

- Focus on what kids do well. Find out about their strengths, and acknowledge that everyone has strengths and weaknesses. People with autism can be exceptionally smart, but our brains are wired a bit differently. It can take me longer to process information. Please always be patient.

- We are all special in our own ways. Our differences make us unique. If you have met one person with autism — you have only met one person with autism! It is a "spectrum disorder," and that means we are all impacted differently and can have different personalities. Oh, and no one "looks autistic." Autism doesn't have an appearance.

- Never underestimate or limit the possibilities of someone because they have autism or any other developmental difference. I was told I would "never" do so many things. I was only three years old then! I was told I'd never have a "meaningful" job. Twenty years later, I have the best job ever as a clubhouse attendant for the 2020 World Series Champion Dodgers.

- Finally, the most important tip I can offer is to always be kind. Kindness rocks!

To RJ, I wouldn't change you for the world,
but I will never stop trying to change the world for you.
To Ryan, Robinson & Roman, the most generous, selfless,
and wholly loving siblings. — HRP

To my mom, Holly. My day one.
Thank you for always protecting my heart.
To my dad and sibs, I love you so much. — RJP

Text copyright © 2022 by Holly Robinson Peete and RJ Peete • Illustrations copyright © 2022 by Shane W. Evans • All rights reserved. Published by Scholastic Press, an imprint of Scholastic Inc., *Publishers since 1920*. SCHOLASTIC, SCHOLASTIC PRESS, and associated logos are trademarks and/or registered trademarks of Scholastic Inc. • The publisher does not have any control over and does not assume any responsibility for author or third-party websites or their content. • No part of this publication may be reproduced, stored in a retrieval system, or transmitted in any form or by any means, electronic, mechanical, photocopying, recording, or otherwise, without written permission of the publisher. For information regarding permission, write to Scholastic Inc., Attention: Permissions Department, 557 Broadway, New York, NY 10012 • This book is a work of fiction. Names, characters, places, and incidents are either the product of the author's imagination or are used fictitiously, and any resemblance to actual persons, living or dead, business establishments, events, or locales is entirely coincidental. • Library of Congress Cataloging-in-Publication Data • Names: Peete, Holly Robinson, 1964– author. | Peete, RJ (Rodney Jackson), author. | Evans, Shane, illustrator. • Title: Charlie makes a splash! / by Holly Robinson Peete and RJ Peete ; • illustrated by Shane W. Evans. • Description: New York : Scholastic Press, an imprint of Scholastic Inc., 2022. | Audience: Ages 4–8. | Audience: Grades K–1. | Summary: Charlie, a boy with autism, describes what his life is like with his twin sister, Callie, who does not have autism, and explains how water — whether in a pool, a tub, or in the aquarium — is like a warm hug that settles him down and calms his mind, allowing him to focus and cope. • Identifiers: LCCN 2021031813 | ISBN 9781338687262 (hardcover) • Subjects: LCSH: Autistic children—Psychology—Juvenile fiction. | Twins—Juvenile fiction. | Brothers and sisters—Juvenile fiction. | CYAC: Autism—Fiction. | Twins—Fiction. | Brothers and sisters—Fiction. | Water—Fiction. | African Americans—Fiction. | BISAC: JUVENILE FICTION / Disabilities & Special Needs | JUVENILE FICTION / Social Themes / Emotions & Feelings | LCGFT: Picture books. Classification: LCC PZ7.P3567 Ch 2022 | DDC 813.6 [E]—dc23 LC record available at https://lccn.loc.gov/2021031813 • 10 9 8 7 6 5 4 3 2 1   22 23 24 25 26 • Printed in the U.S.A.   88 • First edition, August 2022

Shane W. Evans illustrations were created digitally. • The text type was set in Sprocket BT Regular.

The display type was set in F 2 F Mad Zine Whip. • The book was printed and bound at Leo Paper.

Production was overseen by Catherine Weening. • Manufacturing was supervised by Shannon Rice.

The book was art directed and designed by Marijka Kostiw, and edited by Andrea Davis Pinkney.

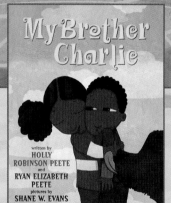

Holly Robinson Peete and her son RJ

PRAISE FOR
My Brother Charlie

by Holly Robinson Peete
and Ryan Elizabeth Peete;
illustrated by Shane W. Evans

"*My Brother Charlie* is a celebration of love and family, and the idea that the things that make us different can be the very same ones that bind us together."
— Al Roker

"One's heart is always in the experiences had with a brother or sister. If you want to know about a person with autism and the impact of autism on a family, this is the book to read."
— NFL HALL OF FAME QUARTERBACK Dan Marino, FATHER OF A SON WITH AUTISM

"*My Brother Charlie* will stand the test of time in the hearts of its readers. Here is a story that rejoioces in what it means to be special."
— Earvin "Magic" Johnson

"As someone who has autism, I'm thankful for *My Brother Charlie*. This is a book every family and classroom should own, whether they've been touched by autism or not."
— Jason McElwain, ATHLETE AND AUTISM ACTIVIST